# MOVED IN!

Timothy Knapman

Loretta Schauer

**LITTLE TIGER PRESS**
London

It was summer but it was raining.
So **Barnaby** was stuck inside
with **NOTHING** to do.

"Read a book,"
said **Dad**.

"Build a rocket,"
said **Mum**.

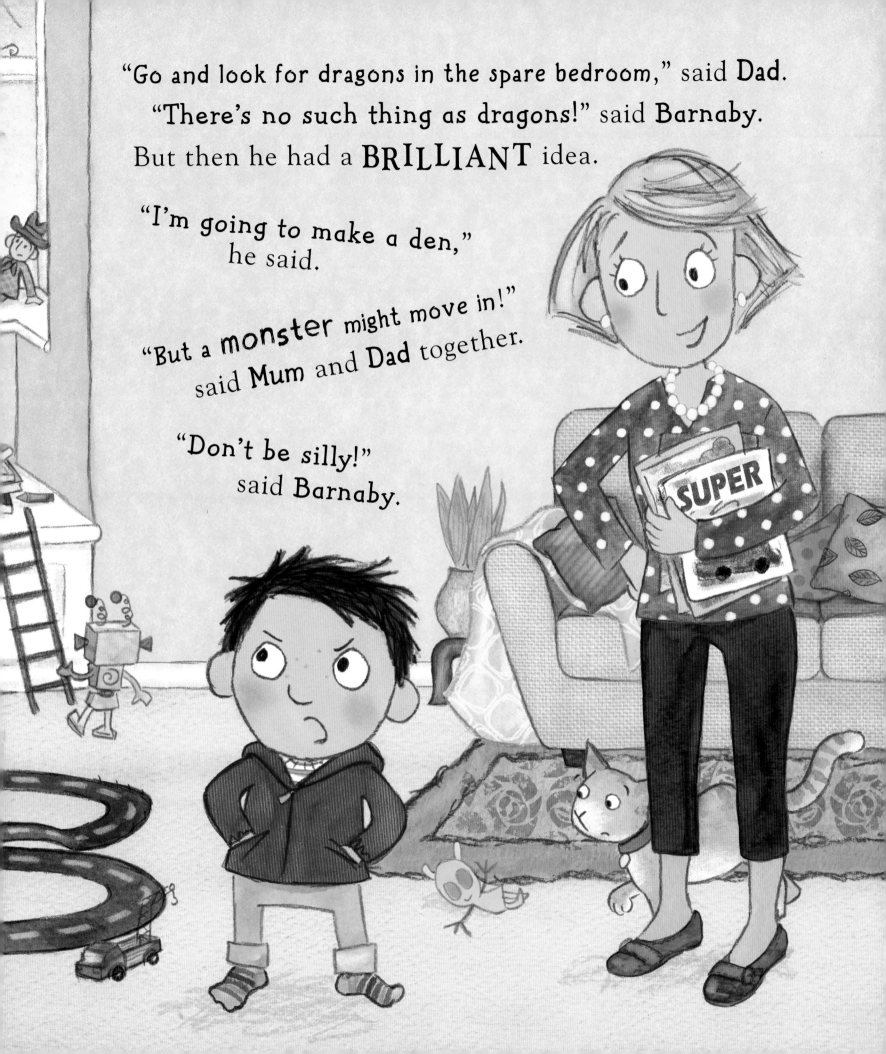

"Go and look for dragons in the spare bedroom," said Dad.
"There's no such thing as dragons!" said Barnaby.
But then he had a BRILLIANT idea.

"I'm going to make a den,"
he said.

"But a monster might move in!"
said Mum and Dad together.

"Don't be silly!"
said Barnaby.

He made an AMAZING den.
It wasn't an outside den made of sticks and dirt and leaves.
You'd expect a **monster** to move in *there*.
It was an inside den, made of cushions
and bits of sofa, with the
rug on top. Far too cosy for

**monsters.**

Still, **Barnaby** got
his ray gun and his
shining armour shield,
**JUST IN CASE.**

But nothing the least bit exciting happened.
It just rained and rained.

Barnaby tried being a
**PIRATE** on the lookout
for ships to plunder . . .

A sword-fighting **KNIGHT**
in his great castle . . .

A **WIZARD** in his cave
of wonders . . .

But it wasn't much fun on his own.
"Sometimes, I wish a monster WOULD
move in!" thought Barnaby.

BIG MISTAKE!

"I don't believe it!"
said Barnaby . . .

"A **monster's** moved in!"

"Told you so!"
said **Mum** and **Dad**.

"Grrr!"
said **Barnaby** crossly.

The **monster** didn't look very fearsome.
His T-shirt said that his name was **Burple**.
So **Barnaby** was brave and
joined him in the den.
"He seems harmless,"
thought **Barnaby**.

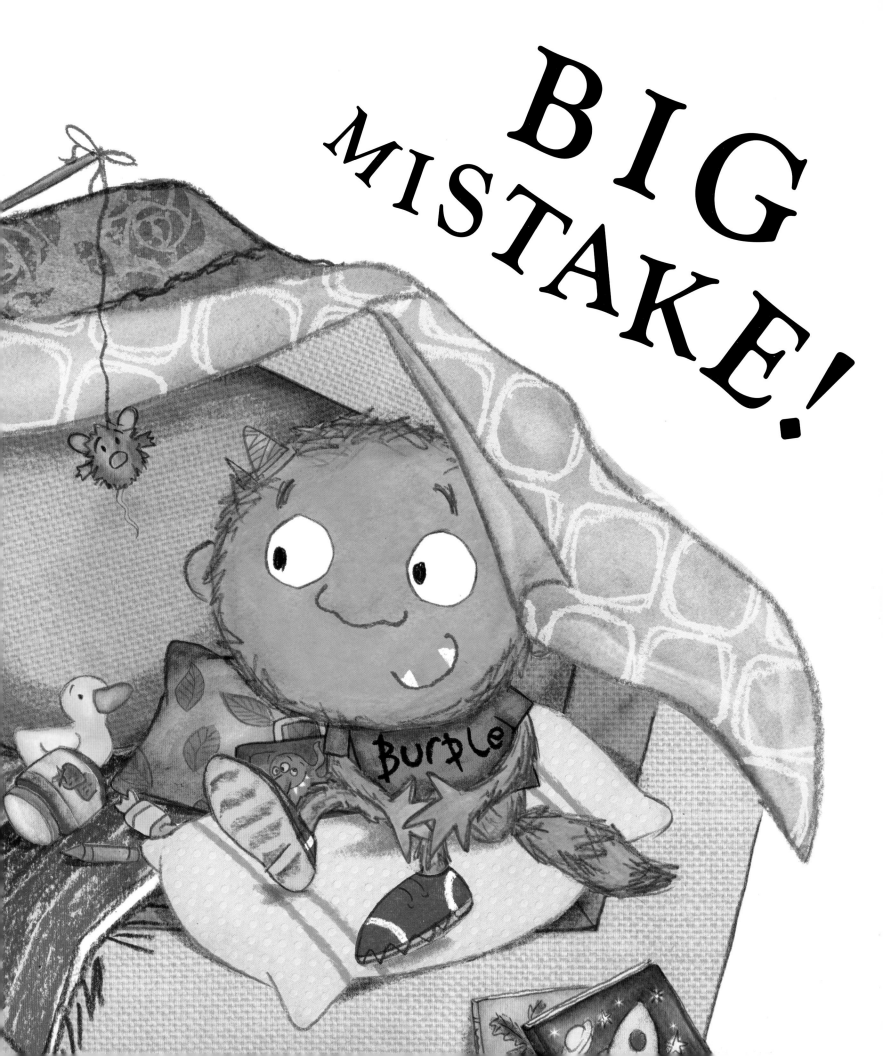

BIG
MISTAKE!

Suddenly **Burple** started

HOWLING

so LOUDLY

that

Barnaby's
ears hurt.

Then

Burple's

DISGU

# STING

PACKED LUNCH escaped
and tried to eat the den.

So they both had to sit on it
until it stopped moving.

"This is no fun at all!"
said Barnaby.

"I'm sorry but it's summer and it's
raining so there's nothing to do,"
said Burple.

That reminded **Barnaby** of
something, and he had a
**BRILLIANT** idea.

He read a book to **Burple**, and **Burple** said, "WOW! Let's read another!"

Then he and Burple built a rocket, and Burple said,

"COOL! Let's blast off!"

And then they went to look for DRAGONS in the spare room.

BIG
MISTAKE!

But when the smoke cleared,
**Burple** said,

"Yay! That was exciting!"

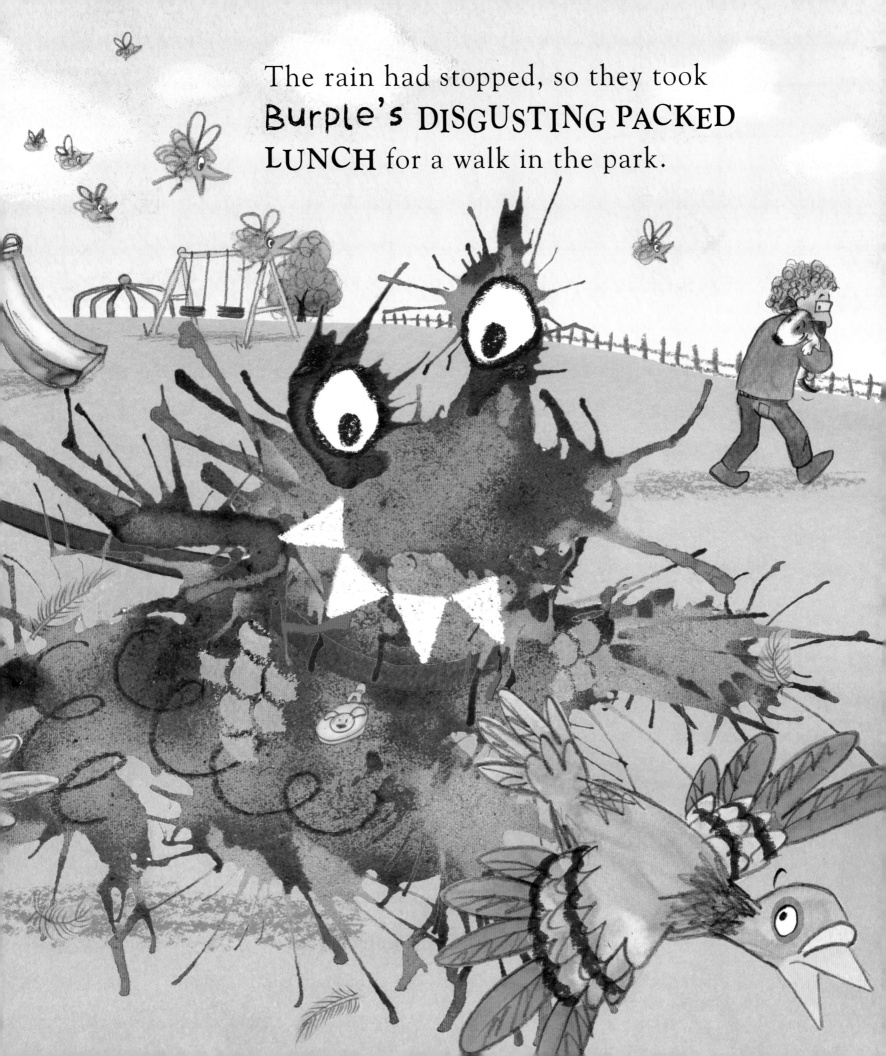

The rain had stopped, so they took **Burple's DISGUSTING PACKED LUNCH** for a walk in the park.

It chased sticks while they hung upside down and told each other jokes. Barnaby and **Burple** laughed so much that their sides hurt.

Barnaby wished **Burple** could stay forever.

But soon it was time
for him to go home.

"This was my best day ever!"
said Burple.

"Mine too," said Barnaby. "Thank
you for coming."

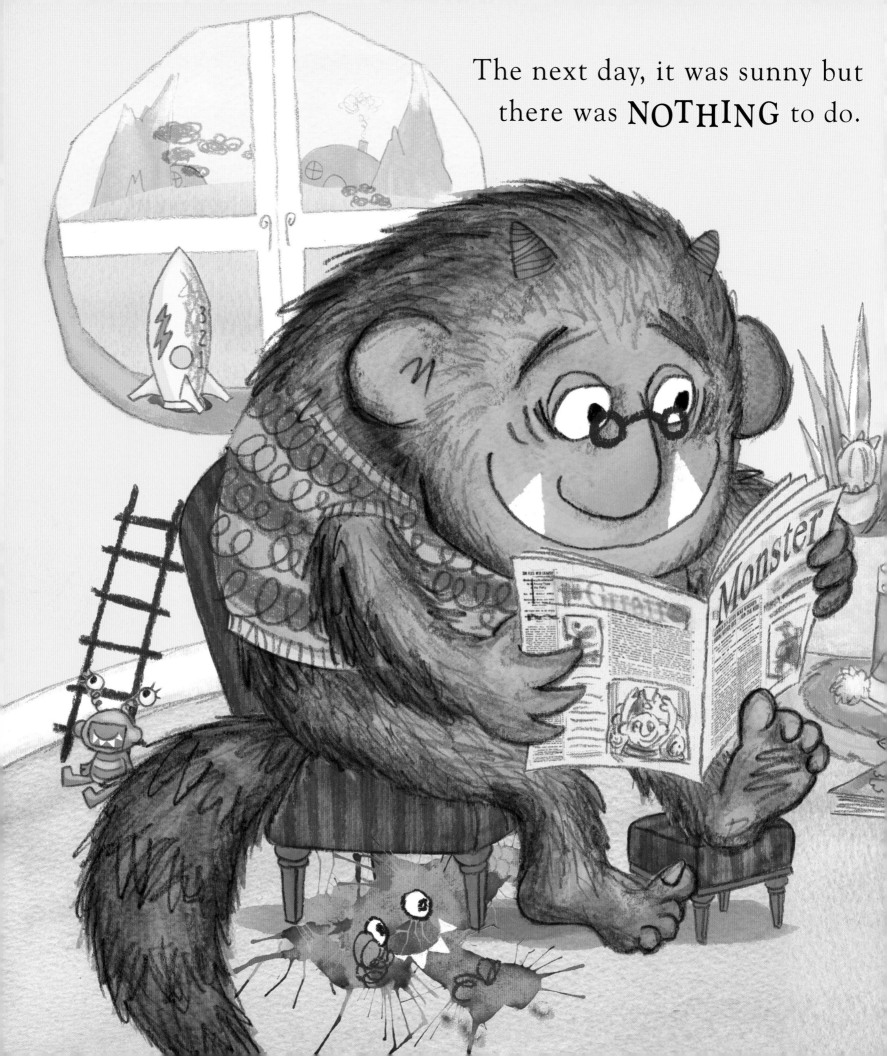

The next day, it was sunny but there was **NOTHING** to do.

And then **Burple** had a **BRILLIANT** idea.

"I'm going to make a den,"
he said.

"But a **boy** might move in!"
said his **Mum** and **Dad** together.

"I hope so!"
said **Burple**.

And he did!